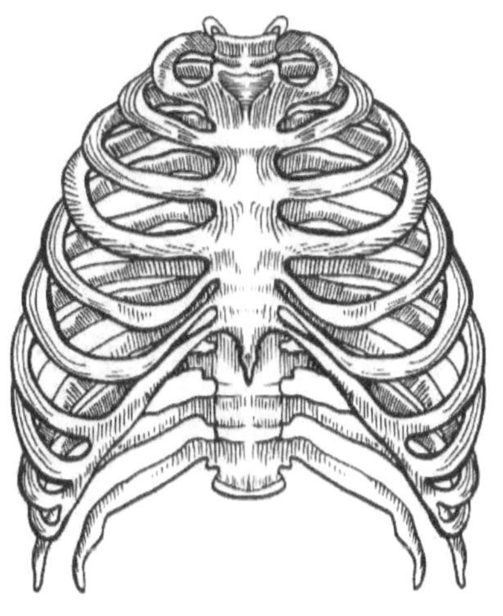

Through my flesh

There are ribs

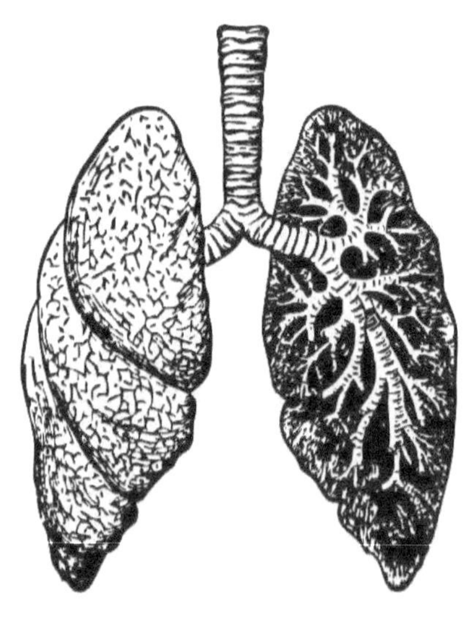

Through my ribs

There are lungs

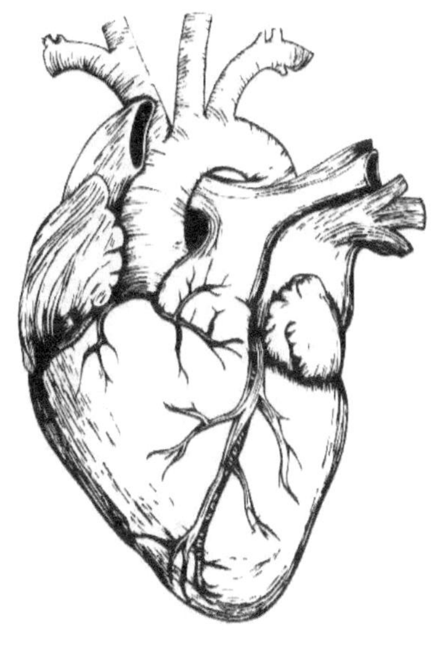

Through my lungs

There are feelings

Through my heart
There are feelings, and they
say;

*Written words turn to mean a lot more
than words said
Well, that's a lie if I tell you...*

For I was told writing isn't always
going to be the solution to express myself
I wrote a hand full of letters to express
my feelings because in front of those I
should be expressing mouthful
I couldn't hear myself perfectly
aligning the words so mystic rapped
together like a Christmas present
But I could hear my heart beating loud
Making me wonder if she could hear it
too
But they never heard it, that's why I
always got rejected
Nor did that dear friend of mine, diary
Like me very much
He always got bored when I always
wanted to talk to him
Via the pen that is
Everything that I've ever written
Dimpho

It's okay to cry

When dark times turn to rise like the
sun
Bleeding the mind and the heart
Breaking your soul and smile
Stealing your love and joy
Destroying your hopes and dreams
It's okay
It's okay to tear up a fountain of bloody
veins on the sleeve
To shout to break down
For pain will never be temporary
As it lasts for eternity
Now you should cry, and hold on to the
pain
For a child in pain, never seeks defeat
As purpose is taught through pain
Hold on just a little bit longer

Open your mind's eye
To see the unforeseen yet seen
While forgotten, nor forgotten while
shadowed by memories of joy
Deep in the dark space where time no
longer grew
But walked yet new but never seen

For that moment
Pain was a friend, never, an enemy
Hold on just a little longer
For days that will come
Tornados, storms, and floods will
occur worse than before
As Matthew said," keep on asking, and
you shall be given"
So does the strength you seek
Shall be uplifted on to you
For beauty in pain
Is beauty for the future
As every thunderstorm that arises
A rainbow shall be at the end
For now, hold on tight
And never let go

Death or life

Concepts webbed in I
As my art of fantasies crumbles
Dust to ashes clueless
Dead alive spiritually
Chest compression by the brain for the
heart
The light you never belong as the dark
too
Return back to I and the world that
rests
A world of bitterness
Bittersweet it is what it offers
A lie sweet as candy, poison in its core
Enjoy its moments until death do us
apart
Cry your eyes out, and let angels come
close
To keep the warmth of your broken
heart with their wings
As your mind's eye sees pain not
temporary
Ride along with
If it never departure, I do apologize
For life itself is never fare upon

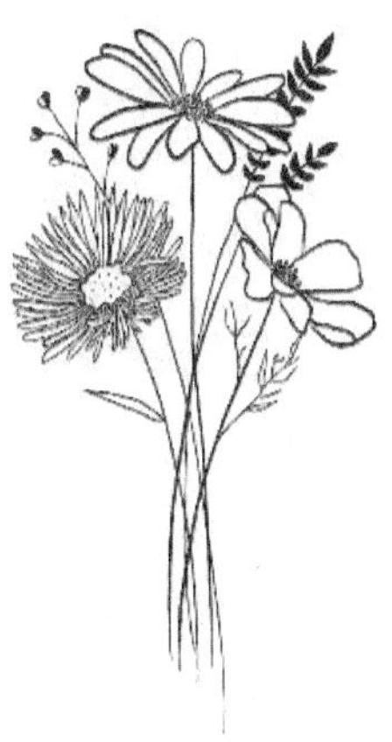

Dear heart
I'm writing you this letter, because I
am tired of the games you play, you bring,
into my life
And I can't stand the pain
I'm just tired of always writing letters
everyday
Just to ease the pain that never fades
Do you even see these tears rolling on
my face every night when I go to sleep
Or do you feel the suffocation taking
control
Taking my breath
I mean I am tired of going outside
Seeing people smiling everyday
Holding hands, enjoying whatever
little they have
What little do I have except nothing
but this emptiness which I'm hoping and
praying every day that it fades
I'm down on my knees asking God for
joy he gives his children

But seems I'm a sinner
Grown up guy waking up everyday
Painted smile on the face
So that he could pretend
While their words sting
While their real joy penetrates the
heart so deep
I can feel myself shaking in despair
Lacking the balance, you bring my
way
I'm trying my best to break out of the
cage
But it seems like I'm locked up

Can you smile for me, then look in the
suspense of them rational critics
For birth was given to a smile that
weakens my heart that binds the twines
and ties the knot
Even if your smile turns to blind
forever worth carved in my obscure

*For my soul craves to witness the
sunshine
For lips that sets sails to worlds afar
With a winding blaze of dark yet lights
up the way to my heart
Mercy, I beg
Not for you to slaughter inches there a
dream of the dreams that dream of you as
twilight never stops to spark careless
whispers from afar as sails waves a mile
apart
Hear the art of heart she gave never
rests in veins in my light*

A smile rare like a lightning ridge
black opal

Ecliptic glimpse of alluring Cassiopeia
Floating seeking infinite in my space continuum
A scenic gaze unfolded to a telenovela
Apollo blessed but the art dispersed
As untailed it lies
Athena gave wisdom to Apollo
Apollo gave blessed desires to I
A prophecy untold nor held
And so, I wrote a scripture
A scripture sculptured by Giovanni Angelo Montorsoli
So, I said heed my warning Leonardo da Vinci
The paint painted such beauty for Mona Lisa
Mona Lisa holds no beauty to my Opal

Love letter

Hi, hope this finds you well

*Sorry about the heading for I do not
know what this letter may be titled to make
your beautiful eyes gaze at it and make you
smile
Most of the time when I bump into
you, you're always having that serious face
I only saw you smile once
and it kind of made my soul follow you
and leave my own body
Now I know why you don't smile often,
your medusa
but instead of turning people into
stone with your crystal eyes, your smile
seems to be the one
So, I must apologize, for this is not a
love letter even though I'm enchanted by
the lady of the skies
I do know that every single person,
even you yourself is taken, if not yet well I
might say that you are booked
Even if you weren't I still don't believe
in such things of beauty and the beast
At this point you might ask yourself
why you should continue reading or what's
the purpose of writing these letter*

Basically, the purpose is to satisfy my heart, a letter or two, for it has been tormenting my brain, torturing it just to think about that smile, those eyes, once the clip has been played the strings on my cheeks turn to pull up, and bring a smile on my face

The only way to remove that clip is to lay down and play clips of dreams

Even though dreams never come true, it's better to dream

In this folded paper of silly things, you found a piece of art

A hand holding a waterlily, on top of the waterlily it's a chrysanthemum flower inside of it, it's a heart

Even though I wish it were a picture of you, I can't draw such beauty on a piece of paper even if try

So, this is were I cut it off, I wish I had the courage to come over to you and say hi, but I don't think I'm man enough to do that

Not because of the 10 stutters I will make just to say hi to you, but because I turn to fall in love easily

*I jump in with my body and soul and
forget the rest its true
So rather than falling in love with a
person, I prefer falling in love with a piece of
paper
If you ever feel like writing back, well I
don't know if I should give you my cupids
number, because I can't give you mine
With the believe that you saw my
cupid, well I don't know you'll find my cupid
I guess*

From

Dimpho

To the girl with the glasses

*Hi, an introduction is one of the
toughest things to write because it needs
time, but unfortunately, its limited at the
moment
I hope this letter finds you well
I know you don't know me and neither
do I, but ever since that day I saw you
coming late to the food processing class, I
think I was star struck or something
With the glasses and the campus
jacket, I had the thought that you are a geek,
by this I mean no offence, just to point out
I like geeks
So, I tried writing this, but I seem to
have forgotten my rhythm, and I just told
myself to forget it
Then I saw you during the BioChem
test*

*Which I tried ignoring, even though
questions arose from my brain asking
myself how sweet your voice sounds, the
type of personality you had and stuff.*
*Which reduced my train of thought
level a little bit, like when I saw you in the
library when I was studying, you were
holding a Rubik's cube, I just said let me try
to write this letter so I can stop this heart
from tormenting my brain about questions
of you*
*And no, I'm not stalking you, I just
bumped into you*
*The weirdest thing is that every time I
bump into you, I can't see your smile, even
when you're with your friends*
*It's weird I guess it adds to your
mysterious and intriguing aura*
*The mysterious girl with the glasses,
when she takes them off, a new world
reemerges*
*This is not a practice of chivalry from I
to you*
It's just me talking

I really wish that I could've came to you and talked to you, but socializing is my weakness, but I'm taking baby steps, and I'm coming along so says people

I know this may sound sudden, since exams are around the corner, but I'm just trying to do myself a favor so my heart can move off from the topic and focus on keeping me alive only

at the moment I would like to remain anonymous hopefully, to put a pin on another fact that I'm not expecting anything from this, as I simply wanted to express my admiration and respect

Sometimes I envy myself
Not the person you see
But the person unseen but only seen
with eyes closed
Felt but never touched in a lifetime
Me, myself and I in my dreams

I envy myself
For the person has everything
Lives in a world were pain is non
existing
Only feels joy and wonders if it is real
He smiles and that smile is not built by
lies but upon sparkles and roses instead of
the cracks spent years perfecting
My soul wants to rip it apart cause the
more I smile the more my soul gets tortured
That's why I spend more time in my
sleep than facing reality

She once asked me
If you wake up tomorrow and were to
never see me again, how would you feel
I told her I would feel nothing

She looked at me with rage
Tears building up in her beautiful
crystal blue eyes
A forged smile she tried to build and
carve to represent her always magnificent
smile
Controlling her temper, what do you
mean
Softly like a newborn kitten calling its
mother
Pain
The love I have for you, is driven by
pain
I turn to love you with my pain
She said how
Confused. With one tear dropping from
her eye forming a river of sadness down her
cheek
I spoke
I will endure all just to make you smile
My pain is your joy
The deeper my feelings for you
excavate my heart into nothingness
When you leave, I'll feel nothing
My brain will cry for you believe that

Torture me with the art gallery your
soul's heart has built in my brain
It will cry when it takes it down
But my heart will be dead
As I put your smile before mine
My pain is your smile

*Can you tell me what you love about
me
And please don't you mention how
happy I make you
Please don't mention how I care about
you
Please don't mention how I express
my love for you
Just tell me what you feel
Don't tell me what you like or what
you liked
I want to know how your heart beats
when my name is called
Don't tell me how you like the way I
present myself to others because those
aren't feelings
Loving how I handle myself
Its loving how I am not who I am
Its loving how I act rather how I live
Its loving the shell that covers my soul
not my soul*

Tell me that you have feelings for me
By looking beneath my eyes

So here I am again
Trying to figure out what to say and
how to save it
I don't want to write something cheesy
to make you think that I have fallen head
over heels for you
Believe me I have but to express it and
tell you is not what I want to do

For they told me never show a girl
your true feelings because they might show
you what a demon looks like
what should I state, that will make the
start smooth
To let your cheeks turn pink
And your eyes glitter like fireworks in
the new year sky
It's of beauty
Just to gaze at you
Watching the butterflies tickle you
While trying your hardest to stand still
But still is impossible
let me write something
Something to make a tear drop from
your eyes

I can write
I can write a thousand poems or
literature for you and still wouldn't be good
enough for you
In my mind I'll always say you deserve
more perfection
More romance

More literature
Or just say I rather be Shakespeare and
speak with perfection when stating my
feelings that are uttered by my soul's heart
enlighten yours
For any single word that I turn to write
Or think to combine
Is always not good enough to awaken
your smile
Even if it does, it still isn't good enough
to me
I'll write off perfection when I think of
you
And only you

I believed it when she told me it was over
She looked at me with the courage of a lion
Eyes gazed in my eyes like she was trying to put some sort of hypnosis

With a heartbeat that was sounding
familiar
I believed it when she told me it was
over
I said OKAY, while trying to hold a tear
from forming a river on my cheeks
Thinking of all the time I've wasted
telling myself that I was doing this for us
I should've but it's this
I knew but my brain shadowed, and
my heart denied it
Feelings never roamed around
And time was never of the essence
Moments were stripped off from
memories
Making them old tales
Leaving me with a question of yet is it
true or not
Don't be surprised
For it
What do you mean by its okay
Do you love me
Why are you saying okay
I need a man to fight for me
Forward is backwards sometimes

Once a decision is made without your
knowledge
It means you weren't included
agree rather to fight
For sometimes some battles need to be
just left on hold

*If only you were the girl, I wish you
were
I'd tell you that I missed you
And say I wish you'd talk to me
Or just miss me too
To think of texting or calling
But your ego is way too high for me to
exist at the top of it
To be one of those that are at the very
peek of it
But I still miss you
Guess I just missed you, even with
your uptight hardheaded self
I wish I could call you, but you
shunned me
Which caught me feeling weak and
stupid
For you shunned me and went to
others you value which I thought I was one
of them
That's why I decided to try and not
think about you
But it seems that I can't
I missed you
And you don't miss me*

All the hours we spent talking when
were just us two
I worthied like pennies passed down
from generation to generation
But I should have guessed that it's a
normal thing for you
You do it more times than I do
But I missed you
I wish I could see you
But I'm trying to lose this emotional
dependence I have for you
I'm trying to kill my own heart for you
In-between a thousand I only thought
of you
I'm trying to kill it, so it won't witness
the era that I'm on in future to history
But I missed you
More than you know
I missed you a lot

*I turn to ask myself if I'm in love with
pain
For that's all I ever feel these days
Gain pain
Even though they say pain is gain
I don't see no outcomes
I'm tired
My mind doesn't want to let me rest as
sometimes I wish it could just stop making
me think about love
Giving me closure to keep on going
Again, and again
I turn to fall for pain
And it's killing my heart
Driving my feelings insane
I'm becoming desperate for love
And I don't want to be
As it might lead me to another
obliterating pain that I never felt before
Destroying my own heart
So, it's better not to love*

Not to trust
Not to gain any relationship
Maybe prefer loose them
For no matter the outcomes
Always bruised
Always forgive and forget
And go back to the same road

*I still ask myself the same question
everyday
Tell someone that you love them
And you need them in your life
because they are the pillar keeping you
standing tall
Nobody can't turn away to see you
shine
With no scars
With no bruises
With no fake smile
But the smile that shines deeper and
brighter than the stars above
Like the sun above
Tell them that you love them
Make them smile
Make them remember your name
when days go by
Telling them that you miss them*

But just a little snap to make you forget
So is it love
Tell if it is
For I still stay up all night and stare at
the night lights above
And ask the universe if you could stay
Will you stay
Turn to hear dark whispers
Turn to wonder what you're doing
What are you happy cause I'm sad
Not knowing how you feel
So is it love
And will it stay

Have you ever sat alone and turn to cry
Have you ever sat alone and turn to
feel this painful sharp pain on your chest as
you cry
As you are deep in thoughts
Listening to music

And that one song took you back
A whole album took you back to the
bad days
Days that you have hidden deep within
your stomach that you thought you
wouldn't have to deal with them
I did
I didn't want to think about it, but it
kept pressing on
I whipped my tears and drank a glass
of water
But they came back bigger than before
The water that I was taking I couldn't
be swallowed
It felt like my lungs forgot how breath
I started feeling blood on my chest
Felt like my heart was dying and now
its bleeding out
I went straight to the mirror and
looked at myself and said never
Never again give my heart to a person
no matter how good they become to me
Never again give my trust to a person
no matter the loyalty they give

*Never again am I going to be taken as
a fool
Never again do I want to feel this
feeling I feel
Never again do I want to associate
myself with people because they always
find a way to destroy one
Mentally, physically, and emotionally
Looking at myself I turn to feel
disappointment that I'm wasting my tears
again
I went straight to bed to calm myself
As the pillow knows all secrets my
tears hold*

I'm alone

I said I am alone
But who cares, nobody
Like nobody is going to care about your
feelings
No matter how sad you are
Your fake smile always fools the
people that are close to you
You got a degree of telling lies and
sculpturing
That's why you lie perfectly and say
you are fine
That's why you sculptured that perfect
smile to fool everybody
The perfect laugh
That perfect giggle with a snort you
make
That's what I know
No matter how many times you cry
Nobody cares
That's the sad part about life
But you can take the pain and shove it
deep down your gut
If it comes out, make sure your alone
So, you can cry a good cry like I do
I mean you already alone

If you cry
If you in pain
If you can't take it no more
I'm sorry and I feel your pain
But that's how we live life
I wish I could say it gets better
But welcome to the world
Were tears are our best friends

10 000 letters
I got 10 000 letters written up in my
brain
But it's hard to tell all out loud
It's even hard to draw them on a piece
of paper
As it seems that my pen has got no ink
I used to have words floating in my
mind
Always looking forward to expressing
all my feelings on top of a beat
Lately I've been silent, and I believe
this silence is killing me
I saw beauty in the presence
And I saw pain in action
I wanted to cry but my tears kept
fighting back
With my eyes telling me it isn't time
and it's not going to happen
I told them please just let me get them
out

My words stuck between my lips
I couldn't talk on the mic
I could talk to the person in my head
telling him that I got
To many words inside my mind
I wish that I could shout them out
I wish that I could write them
But it seems
I have reached 10 000 letters in my
heart
Now I'm dead inside
I wanted to cry
But I was too busy to cry
Putting my hearts pain into work
Every time I would record a song about
it
I end up turning it down
As fear lurks beneath my feet of the
critics
They told me pain is virtue
Well yes, I can tell you that pain hurts
I still visit them
10 000 letters I wrote

Nights turned to days have passed
Yet every single day that passes
I witness pure devastation
An apocalyptic era

Were all butterflies are no longer
shimmering with beauty
Giving me kisses with their wings in
my stomach
But they are turned into zombies
holding riffles
Spitting bullets like a massacre in my
heart
Why you may ask
Cause I'm back in the same spot of
missing you
Where in my heart my feelings
Are at war with the butterflies

Do you know the story of beauty and
the beast
Have you seen it
I know it's just a movie
A fairytale made to give people like me
hope
To be with people like you
And I know my words are called out as
spared change like the coins in my pocket
Causing holes in them
But can me and you just bring the
fairytale into reality
For I know I don't have the standards
to match yours
But I have the love to give
And its excess for you
So, will you?

*Is it okay to take notice of your smile
first
More than your beauty
Is it okay for me to take notice of your
eyes second
Before your own soul
For your whole body I do not care off
But the smile from you is what I seek
And the constellated eyes of yours are
what show me the way
A way to your heart
So, it can be just I and you
I know looking at my face you might
say its lies
Looking in my eyes you might be
confused
But I'm not at all as I seem
Trust in your heart please
Even though it turned against you at
times*

Guess it's true what they say
I'll never be good enough for love
For as times I seek
Times I wasted trying to find the
perfect match for me
A matchstick is what I receive
That touches my heart in flames
For days I've stayed in the bliss
Waiting...
And waiting...
How long should I wait
For I know they say let love find you
I've been feeling so lonely my heart is
crumbling
No tears, coming out my eyes
As I've cried them all
Cause the pain is too much to bear

*It's time for me to set sails to a wonder
land
A land where everything is possible
A place where all dreams are real
As the biggest dream ever made by I
Was for I to be with you
With you I am with as I slowly close
my eyes
And drift away
I can never complain
For even though it hurts me the most
to see you smile with another
Another which is I smile wider than
before when with me*

I tried to smile today
My brain could but my heart couldn't
As the void in my heart is deep
Like quicksand you'll never know
where it goes
It leads downwards that's for sure
I opened the door to go outside
Got greeted by many smiles with
people walking with friends and their
partners
I tried to smile but Mr. Loneliness
popped in front of my face
A fist that flew straight to my gut
Ached like a brain freeze
My friend sadness hugged me from
behind and whispered in my ear
Close the door
Let's go dream about a better place
Than what you see before you
As the door starts to squirm and crack

Locked
Everything feels at peace

Hi

Have you ever missed someone
Someone you never knew but talked
like you knew each other

*What happens if that conversation
stops
And one of you had nobody but her
By one of you I mean I
By had nobody I mean catches some
feelings
For I've been perusing through the
internet in hopes that I might see that
angelic face I missed and longed for
For everyday it has been her roaming
in my mind
I know it's my fault
I got lost in the glimpse and glimmers
of these world
So did she too
Now the only problem which arises
Causing immediate obliteration
Is when I find her, what would I say
"I miss you"
Would she think about the days me
and her had
Special moments we shared, tell her I
felt her
What will it lead too*

*Cause what if she moved on and found
people better than me
Should I just live with her as a memory
Haunting me in every thought
For I'm scared too
To even try to tell her how I feel*

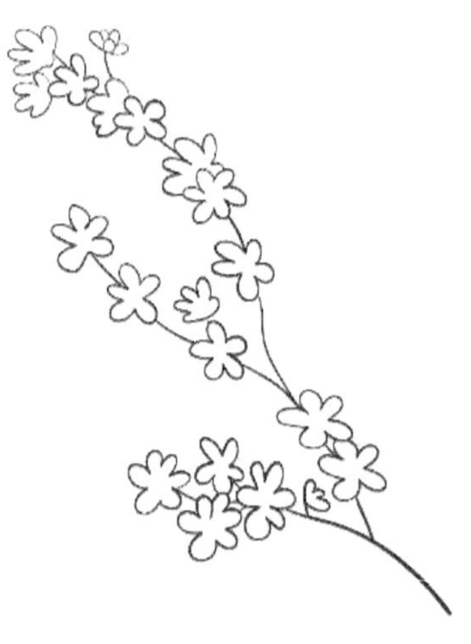

I told you that I love you

You told me that I'm wasting my time
It's been years since I uttered a word
on you
But every day it has been said
It's like spring everyday you're in my
thoughts
Even though the words you have said
have carved a huge scar in my heart
Does it pain
No
For this scar reminds me of you
And the smiles you brought on my
face
Now you're all grown
And beauty God gave a hand full
A dozen of boys from charming to
prince are all behind your tail
For you have put them on a spell that
took them all by default
To me it's just a phase
I should wait till your all done
Those are the only words I can say to
make me feel better
Words to prevent this book from being
wet with all of my tears

The only fear I got is that
I can be patient enough
To find out that someone has stolen
your heart

Dear Heart
21st of January 2023
10:57 a.m.
Hello
I hope you're doing well
And the scars you felt and dealt with
are all better
It's me, the soul
I wrote to you this letter to tell you that
finding a soulmate is not easy
So please I beg of you
Stop falling in love with those who are
not the one
For the soulmate will be found by I
first
Then Mr. Brain will analyze if she is
the one
And if she is
We will give her to you Mr. Heart
But for now, please be at ease
For it hurts me to see you hurt and
bruised by those who are not
I hope you get to read this letter

And feel what I feel
Yours sincerely
The soul

Is it okay to tell you that I love you
Should I whisper it into your ears so it
could send shivers through your soul
Should I shout it out on top of the
tallest building in the world
So, the heavens can hear me saying
the three magical words that bind us
together
So, they can bind us even more
Is it okay for me if I kiss you
Those strawberry lips that sparkle like
diamonds that crystal up in the sky
Or should I just turn on the speaker
and listen to our favorite songs
As it plays sweet melodies as you are
resting on my chest listening to your
heartbeat
Staring at you
For sometimes
It's hard to believe that I am...

In reality
That this is real
For I have found love

I know
I know
I'm stupid for falling in love with you
Without you feeling the same way
about me
But it's not my fault
If you want to blame someone
Please
Blame my heart and brain
For every time I tried to erase you from
my mind you keep on coming back
Haunting me
Every single day
And what's even worse is because I've
put my all in you
So, what else must I do
Get a heart transplant so my heart can
beat for someone else

Get a brain surgery so I can think
about something else besides you
What shall do

Can you say something
Any word at all
To make my feelings rise like the
sunshine
As its brightness my smile
Making my cheeks turn red
Please give me sun lotion

So, I could smile even more
Just give me that little thing
A word or letter
A giggle or a smug
Just so I can fly
As my words cut short
And the butterflies in my stomach lift
me up
Up
To the heavenly skies

If you wanted to talk to me
You could've said so
I would have given you a chance

Because everybody deserves a chance
I know pride sometimes likes to take
over
Take control
Sometimes ego likes to make some
threats
And fear
Always exaggerate things
We can overcome all of that
But never at once
Those three friends we all have
Don't have to be the only ones who
control you
Rather
Be mostly friends with your deepest
desire

So, like is it okay for me to cry for you
Cause my mother told me to never cry
on you

And never about you
I feed my brain with so many lies
Just to look at you makes me want to
die
The worst pain I feel is when I picture
you with another guy
Even though I tried my best to make
you mine
Is it love I feel
Cause I'm hoping
it may not be hatred
As I clearly told my heart and soul that
I'm fine
I've accepted defeat

Stars up in the sky

A wish I made from my heart
Where is the fairy to make you mine
Cause Geppetto wished for a boy
And you showed up
And gave him Pinocchio
And he rejoiced
And still I'm wishing for her
Her smile only
But you've given me emptiness
and nothing rhymes with emptiness
Except a moment of sadness
A moment without happiness
Is not what...
I was hoping for
It's just a poetic love
Notes written by the heart
When ever considered to matter in this
dark world
As I still sing
Twinkle Twinkle little stars
Where is my wish I wished from the
heart

I know you don't see me as a men of
your dreams
Just only if you knew that dreams
don't always come true
That's why we settle for less
And truly speaking I'm that less
But still
You won't take notice of me
As I stare in your eyes
Never in person but your pictures your
videos
I glare at those eyes
That show no sights never seen
Stars never shinned
Stories never told
While your lips take me to a journey of
untold folklore
Myths from riches to diamonds
In which I believe
But I'm just trying to put you in my
head before I set sail
To the ocean
For its you who's going to save me
As my medicine

So many wishes I made
So many times, I tossed coins in the
wishing well just for you to look at me twice
So many nights I've laid wide awake
waiting to see just the shooting star
Just to make you mine
With the coldness of the night
breaking my bones
With the darkness calling my name
Screaming out words I cannot
pronounce
It's just a wish I know
But only if only
I'll just get this one wish

Hii
Is it okay if I utter a few words
A few words that echoed deep in my
heart
I know the sun has set and risen as
birds flied past
As the days these days fly past without
setting sight
But today I managed to lasso the sun
So that it doesn't set without me
uttering these few words
Words that are penniless to you
But riches for me
Do you still remember me
In hopes you do please do as I beg of
you
Just a memory bad or good
One or two
Of me and you

So, these words I utter can bring back
the memories shared
As they say SpongeBob

I know they told you your beautiful
A small validation that made you high
in cloud 9

*Beauty attracts beauty that's what you
believe
For that simple validation made us
split
I never told you your beautiful
Nor no such words will be said from I
to you
For that simple validation
Made you take a separate path
And forget about the path we both laid
together
Beauty attracts beauty
The necessity of I with you was
destroyed
For beauty I don't posses
But beauty of the heart I gave
That's why I never said your beauty
Yet in my eyes are my soul stares at
yours
Beauty is a word that underrates your
stars
But since beauty in validation took you
by default
The word beauty perfectly describes
you*

For your soul no longer is underrated
by the word beauty
As it suits you perfectly as desired by
you

Hey

It's me, your secret admirer

I hope you're doing well and spent your weekend well playing netball in the garden of heaven with other angels. And yah you top them all. I spent my weekend in hell, I *lost my phone which has almost all my entire memories but at least my feelings for you are still here in my heart. Yes, they didn't steal them Cause my heart and soul held them tight and hard. I hope you read my first letter lying on your bed listening to love songs smiling and blushing again and again like Hazel Grace smiling with Augustus. That's what I do when I write a letter for you, some say I'm crazy, watch a lot of movies, worst part they are saying I'm gay cause I can't express my feelings with a girl or anyone. Me gay imagine it; can you believe it.*

I mean if I was gay, I wouldn't have a crush on you right now, writing you letters. And the clips of you smiling and laughing wouldn't be stuck in my brain in slow motion playing in auto repeat. And in-between all the saga of being like all weird is that the fault in our stars taught me to always try to spend time with a person you truly value which is you for me. Hazel said," Some infinities are longer than others, but at least I got to spend my infinity with you". So, like she meant in-between 1 minute to 2 minutes there are infinite numbers and in-between 2 minutes and 3 minutes there are infinite numbers as well. But the infinity of 1-2 minutes is smaller than that of 2-3 minutes. That's the phrase of some infinity's are bigger than others. So Ayanda I wouldn't mind spending infinity with you as the poem I wrote for you says:

<u>A moment with Ayanda</u>

The poem goes on, but you get the point. But the one thing that I wish to do Its to slow dance with you. I think about it, daydream about it, dream about it and it's never leaving. There's something about slow dancing that I find interesting like deep eye contact, where my soul seems to be intertwined with yours for a moment in time and the heart of I, and you, beating the rhythmic beat of perfect harmony. And who better to do it with besides you. Hope I'm not freaking you out. And yes, we might be in the same class and doing the same course, but I wouldn't be affecting anything cause for me when I think of a relationship, I think of couple's goals, like *me and you competing, working together for preparation of tests, joking about our marks and damn your smile. Will be like the joker and Haley queen*

So yeah, I really like you and have strong feelings for you. And I'd love to know you better instead of lying to myself thinking you like natural hair or something like sometimes if things start getting better and I man up to talk to you we can go on dates, parks just to know each other if you fine with it no rush

So, for now a couple of things you should know is that "kaswa "it's hard for me to talk to girls and tell them face to face how I feel. I can't express myself well but slowly for you I'll do it, I like reading novels, I'm a writer, editor, poet greatest even I love watching movies classic romance like Bonnie and Clyde, beauty and the beast, titanic and etc., comedy, sci-fi a little, animation and cartoons. Sports I play tennis and cricket. Yah, I think I should end it here. So, Julieta, what do you think?

Hope you get to read this

Yours truly D
X.O.X.O

Hi

I wish it were easy to say that in front of you, without my heart pounding hard and wildly on my chest. I'm not sure, for whether I was daydreaming or not, for the first time I gazed at you, I was blinded by the astonishment of this sculptured physique laid in front of I. let those that say love at first sight is dull, might have been enchanted by the mid evil spells. For I seem to be struck by a love arrow, from the cupids, gods of love. I know where it struck me, but my cupid is clumsy and a little bit childish. I might ask it to shoot you down with a love arrow, but its clumsiness' might cause it to miss, like all the targets it missed.

Anyway, I do possess some questions for the lady that these concerns. When did you departure from the heavens, and what was your mission, that made God to send you on earth in order to accomplish. For the sight I set on you doesn't want to go blur nor grey dissolved in the lake of past emotions. If not from the heavens, then no such creature can reside on earth with such beauty.

Maybe I might be dreaming, but hopefully I may not. But I have to apologize to the lady from the heavens, for unfortunately, I must cut this short. Time is needed for I to learn more about thou, and let my heart rest at ease, for it has been beating at full tilt than normal.

So, for now I bid you adieu, see you when you see me, but you won't, so, see me not thy see you

From Dimpho

Greetings to the lady of the skies.

As I write this letter, my mind hasn't been resting at ease like it was foretold. For you seem to be hunting me through the night's world of fantasies, and I so fear, that you might be the hero of this untold folklore. A folklore which I believe will only be, but never a story of reality.

Even so lady of the skies.

Let me not sadden myself, with words that only cut deep but rather picture your smile and let all my worries and troubles fade away. For I do not know why the Mona Lisa was painted, for Leonardo da Vinci would have dreuled the same as I, as I laid my eyes on you. Perfection, at its peak, like they say in French, "une femme est plus belle que le monde ou je vis, et je ferme les yeux". So, I to, let my eyelids take the pleasure, in closing to picture this picture painted perfect of the lady of the skies.

Hopes do turn to approach the mind. For you to smile brighter than the sun, but I pray for your smile not to blind me. For I still long to see what the crystal ball shows of the future. Let me not jinx it, nor let me not hear

*what's been said or seen but see with mine
than theirs nor mine of ears.*

*Roses black or red, clover crystal or blue,
shine your cheeks for I.*

From: Dimpho

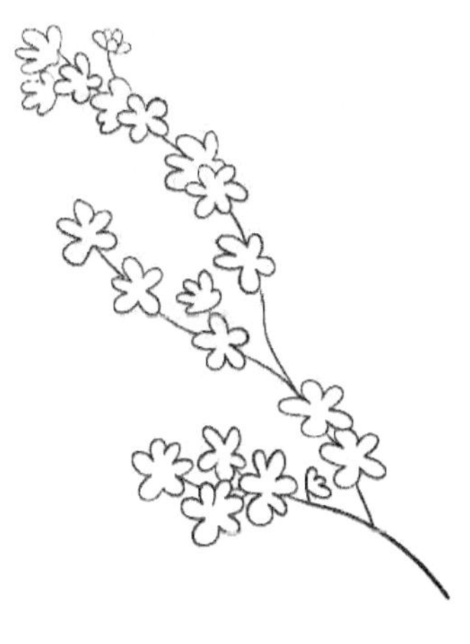

Hi

I still remain speechless

Stuttered words only float around my throat, as much as I try to yell them out. The silent cry of the cold winter child remains. Do wishes really turn to be true, for my deepest desire it's you, nothing more nor less. For with you, I do feel worthy of being a ruler, all possibilities do arise from north to south.

Damaged inside, I am, but lessons never taught of love, one wish, to erase all wishes, one wish for my heart to beat a drum of harmony while in thought of you, not banging sounds of thunder.

How can one turn to try to live, as his own life revolves around the other. Broken I am, to pieces I remain. For every single love song makes me daydream about the future of I and you. Of how I terminated, brutalized and murdered my own dreams with a skill, ability I so desired for once to make thou mine. In turn left me in ashes of ash trays, my deepest desire, gone but still here. It pains me the most as I cannot utter a word of the butterflies that seem to be turning evil biting and ripping out my fleshed skin of my heart. Blood does bleed.

One wish I just wished, for thy to be mine forever to hold dear in thy heart. But for all it is but a dream. A wish only comes to those who only work for it, enslaved myself to labor no human has seen with their own two eyes. And still nothing, as my hands turn to bleed, my eyes tearing my soul up like dinner plate for scavengers. Tired I remain, but still afraid, for my feelings might disappear before they share a drink of champagne under the beautiful dark star moon night.

From the heart

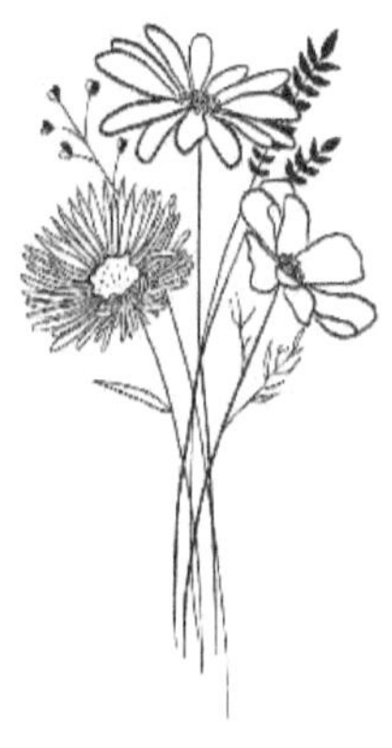

Doesn't it hurt?
Isn't I killing myself.
While awake I stare at the ceiling.
For a tear to drop to cool my feelings.

But for what which drop represent I remain clueless, for countless of times I was bid adieu, yet my soul's heart is still affixed. Dear lord I begged for a love portion for only I and her. Drunk by I alone, with a spirit that never peeks to see my cheeks seasonal reddening like a peach. For the love portion in plans, was never for thy alone but thou as well. A dream I saw far away, collapsed to pieces to so rest in peace to my heart, for in pieces you remain.

You remain in pieces, and dead for the living has risen with dawn. a thousand pieces synchronization of a melodic beat for thy, why did I burden myself with love when itself doesn't show a sweat of care. Tears turn to rise, as the veins slither like serpents to drink the pain. Should I burn the bits of pieces of my soul's heart to ashes? For ashes to ashes seem to be better than dead to live and have no love while beating outrageously for it. Conflicted as I may, the pain I see, it's an ocean blue.

Thoughts of dots of lots of roots, tangled like Veins leading me straight to

*treasure I for seek for eons. A journey that
left me, dressed in
black and blue, to a prize that has
already been claimed. So, thy should drink a
bottle tip to toe, shall the love never received
send me to the heavens with its cravings, or
shall I forever remain wailing, drowned in a
pool of regret. For I stare to watch from afar,
as joy is brought to the treasure and the
hunters, even though my eyes seem to fall
out. The breath I breath becomes clouded
with red hot bitterness of fire*

Every day you turn to smile.
Tell yourself that it will be alright.
A smile does pop, but gets eradicated
in seconds like an ad.
Smiling wide like earth is a fantasy.
One step that changes your day to a
nightmare.
A day spent like any other.
Hallow and dark with no silver lining.
Numb I feel, or pain I feel.
I can't lock myself up in a house of
cards for eternity.
For I to, do need to feel the joy.
Down on my knees as I remain.
With tears that darken my own soul.
For I don't know what my own sins
are.
Yet still I do know that I'm not
innocent.
And forgiveness is what I ask.
Is this punishment of a lifetime?

*For I can bear to witness a day with
this pain.
A child I still remain, like any other in
this world.
Mercy, I beg, for I know nothing of
what I am doing.
A curse, of my own doing
As my heart pounders in pain, while
my chest darkness as it caves in.
Love me not, I remain the same.*

100 reasons why I love you-for Ayanda

1. *I love your smile*
2. *I love your eyes*
3. *I love the way your cheeks remind me of my young self being called tumtum*
4. *I love your voice*
5. *I love your personality*
6. *I love the way I feel near you*
7. *I love your generosity*
8. *I love the way you make me so happy*
9. *I love the way you encourage me to work hard without saying anything, only by just looking at you*
10. *I love the way you make my soul dance*
11. *I love the way you're so focused in class*
12. *I love your obsessive-compulsive personality disorder*
13. *I love the fact that you're a hard-working person*
14. *I love your weird walk "my favorite actually"*
15. *I love the way you take care of yourself*
16. *I love the way you respect and know who you are in life*

17. I love the way you bring a smile to my face

18. I love your innocent look

19. I love your angry / serious face "2nd best favorite thing "

20. I love your child friendliness

21. I love the relationship you have with other people

22. I love the fact that you are always happy

23. I love the hatred you make me feel for not telling me that your sad

24. I love the fact that you are a believer

25. I love the way you pop up in my mind like an ad in bad times and good times

26. I love your smart looking good girl physique

27. I love your smartness

28. I love the fact that I know what unconditional love means from you

29. I love your strong faith in God

30. I love your honesty

31. I love the fact that you share your problems with your journal

32. *I love the fact that you care about others*

33. *I love the fact that you always have a plan b*

34. *I love the fact that you're always trying to be strong to numb the pain*

35. *I love the fact that you love my poetry*

36. *I love the fact that my heart melts like chocolate when I picture you in my mind or watch your videos*

37. *I love the fact that you make me want to do anything for you*

38. *I love your cute laugh, kind of like a giggle*

39. *I love your kind heart*

40. *You mean a lot to me*

41. *I love the way your presence lifts me up*

42. *I love how you say you'll pray for me*

43. *I love the way your lifestyle changed mine*

44. *I love how I see a future with infinite possibilities*

45. *I love your sense of style*

46. I love the way you understand the way I'm feeling

47. I love the way that you consider other people first than you

48. I love how you make me feel like you're my soulmate

49. I love how you make me feel like I'm human

50. I love the fact that your humble

51. I love your little big old turkey neck

52. I love the little details of who you are

53. I love the fact that you own responsibility

54. I love the feeling of loneliness and sadness I feel when your absent

55. I love the guilt you make me feel when a day passes without seeing you

56. ...

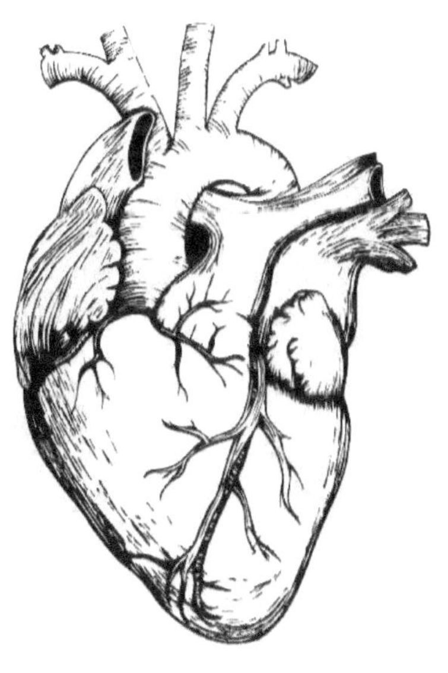

From feelings to the heart

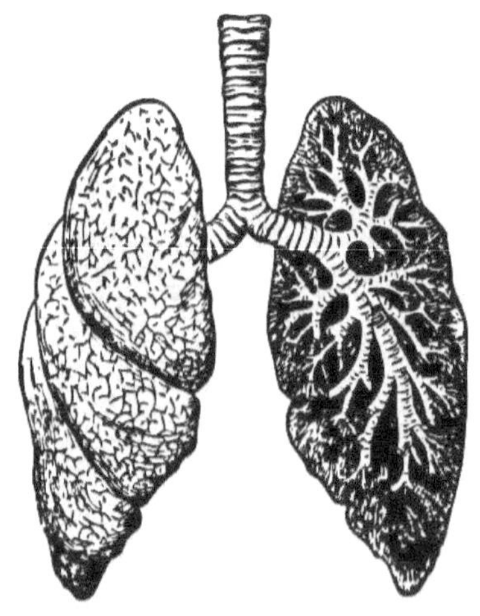

From my heart to lungs

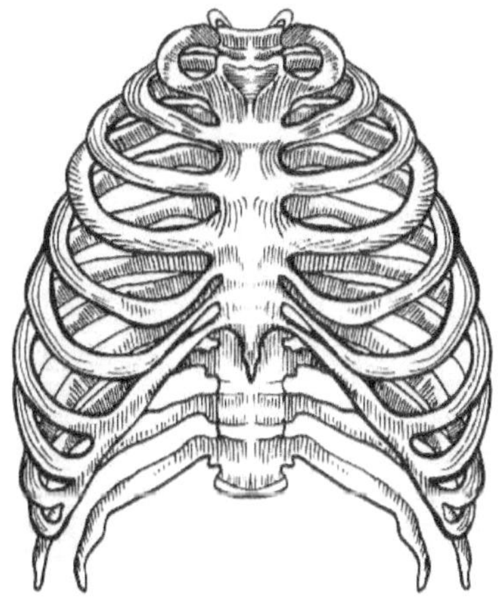

From lungs to ribs
My flesh is I
Silent I remain
As the ink on my pen speaks for I